Tales from the Brothers GRIMM

Retold by

ROBERT MATHIAS

Illustrated by

Paul Bonner

Silver Burdett Company
Morristown, New Jersey

Published 1986 by
Hamlyn Publishing
A division of The Hamlyn Publishing Group Limited,
Bridge House, London Road, Twickenham, Middlesex, England

Published in the United States in 1986
by Silver Burdett Company,
Morristown, New Jersey

Copyright © 1986 Text and illustrations
Robert Mathias, Publishing Workshop

Set in Monophoto Baskerville by Servis Filmsetting Limited, Manchester

ISBN 0-382-09259-7

Library of Congress Cataloging-in-Publication Data

Mathias, Robert.
  Tales from the brothers Grimm.

  Contents: Snow White — The robber groom —
Tom Thumb — [etc.]
    1. Fairy tales—Germany. [1. Fairy tales.
  2. Folklore—Germany] I. Kinder- und Hausmärchen.
  II. Bonner, Paul, ill. III. Title.
  PZ8.M44873Tal 1987   398.2'1'0943   86-3864
  ISBN 0-382-09259-7
  Printed in Spain

Contents

Snow White

IT WAS THE MIDDLE OF WINTER and broad flakes of snow were tumbling and swirling around in the cold night air. Dark shadows crept into every nook and cranny and stood out sharply against the pale silver glow reflected from the moonlit snowdrifts. The small creatures of the forest had taken refuge, huddling deep in their nests far below the frozen shroud that lay across the land.

High on a hill above the ice-latticed treetops stood a castle. It rested like a great black rock amidst the gleaming whiteness that surrounded it. Its turrets and walls were dark and gloomy in the creaking chill, blind save for a solitary golden glow high up in one corner of its ebony façade. The glow came from a tiny window and it flickered like a dying star as the snowflakes danced past it.

Close by the window sat a queen quietly sewing and looking out over the frosty scene. She had a child within her whose birth was near, but despite the joy this brought her, there was a sadness in her heart. As she measured her stitches she prayed for strength, for the cold of the long winter had entered her bones and she felt frail and weak.

Suddenly, she started, as the sharp needle pierced her finger and three drops of blood fell on to the snow-covered windowsill. She gazed thoughtfully at the crimson stains coloring the white snow and her sad eyes filled with tears.

"Would that my child be a daughter with skin as white as that snow, with cheeks as rosy red as blood and hair as ebony black as the window frame."

Outside the wind gusted wildly and the long night wore on.

The good queen died but her child was, indeed, a daughter. The queen had died that the child should live, but just before she closed her eyes for the last time she saw that her wish had come true – the child's skin was as

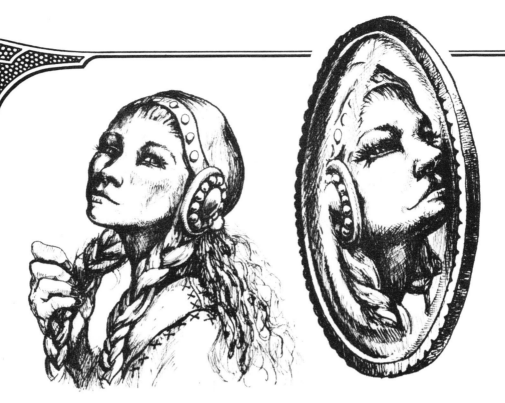

fair as driven snow, her cheeks were rosy blood-red and her shining hair was as black as ebony. The queen's lips had trembled; "I will call her Snow White," she murmured.

The king, though saddened at his wife's death, married again and took for himself a woman of a different nature. His new queen was tall and beautiful, but her heart was cold and her pride extreme. She would spend hours attending to her appearance and scold her maidservant cruelly if her hair was not just right. She dressed in the finest robes and her vanity was such that each of her fingers was adorned with precious stones of jet and sapphire. Her arrogance was so great that she could not bear to think for a minute that anyone could surpass her in beauty or charm. Each day she gazed at her reflection in her mirror – it was a magic looking-glass and she would speak to it.

> *"Tell me, mirror, tell me true,*
> *Of all the fair maids in the land,*
> *Who is the fairest? Tell me who?"*

And the mirror would answer,

> *"Thou, queen, that before me stand,*
> *Art the fairest in the land."*

But as time went by and the years passed, Snow White grew to be more and more beautiful. By the time she was seven years old she was as bright as the morning sunshine, her ebony hair glistened about her pure rosy-cheeked face and fell around her snow-white shoulders. She was equally as beautiful as any maid throughout the land and certainly as fair as the queen herself.

The queen became cold and distant to the child and treated her with scorn. Inside her cruel heart she nurtured a hatred for the girl's sweet nature and beautiful form. At last there came a day when her worst fears were realized: as was her habit she had gone to consult her magic mirror and was astonished by its reply.

> *"Thou, queen, may fair and beauteous be,*
> *But Snow White is lovelier now than thee."*

The queen could not believe her ears and repeated her question again and again, but the mirror's answer remained the same.

> *"Thou, queen, may fair and beauteous be,*
> *But Snow White is lovelier now than thee."*

Instantly the queen flew into a rage and her frenzied anger was so fearsome that her terrified maid fled from the chamber. Seething with envy the queen sent for her groom. He stood before her, nervously shuffling his feet as he listened to her cruel plan. Her fury boiled over and she paced back and forth with her eyes blazing, spitting out her words with unconcealed venom and hatred.

"You will take her from my sight!" she screamed. "Into the darkest depths of the forest . . . and there you will cut her throat! Be sure to do your work well and see that I never set eyes on her again!"

The groom hurried fearfully from the queen's evil presence lest she turn her spite on him. Straightaway he took Snow White from the castle and led her deep into the forest.

They walked for a long time and it began to get dark; the groom bade her sit down and rest. He sat a little apart from her and slumped sadly against a tree resting his head in his hands and shaking it worriedly. The weight of his duty was heavy on his conscience; during their long walk Snow White's good nature had charmed him and her soft smile had made him pity her. He told her of the queen's command, and of his fear of being punished if he should fail. Now his heart was full of sadness and he couldn't bring himself to carry out the wicked orders. He rose and came close beside her; resting his hand on her shoulder he said: "No! I will not slay thee!" He had made up his mind. "I'll take my chances with the queen's displeasure – I'll let her think that you are dead and keep my silence.''

Snow White thanked him for his kindness in sparing her life and he turned and walked off quickly down the path.

Snow White was alone in the dark forest. She found a hollow beneath a great oak tree and crawled inside to try to sleep. All around her the night closed in and strange somber shadows flitted between the thick trees. She listened to the fearful night sounds of the forest and trembled for her life – a deep throaty growl nearby told her that wolves were about. She saw them approach and her alarm grew, but they stopped and sat close by, like silent sentinels, and did not molest her. At last, overcome by exhaustion, she fell into a troubled sleep.

She woke as something prodded against her left cheek, she opened her eyes and found a fawn nuzzling against her. The wolves had disappeared and the sun was high above the treetops. Dancing shafts of light filtered through the interwoven branches over her head and warmed her face. She smiled and reached out to pat the dappled fawn but her movement startled it and it scampered away. Birds were singing in the trees and somewhere out of sight she could hear the busy chattering of squabbling squirrels. Cheerfully she picked herself up and set off through the green sunny forest.

Late in the afternoon she began to feel hungry and looked around to see if there were any berries growing near that she might eat. Peering this way and that she suddenly saw a tiny cottage almost completely hidden by the thick bushes. Had she not been looking closely, she wouldn't have seen it at all, for it stood tucked within a shady hollow in the center of a neatly trimmed clearing. It was surrounded on all sides by tall silvery birches and broad-girthed beech trees.

Snow White went up to the door and knocked – there was no answer so she went inside. The room she found herself in was neat and tidy and a long table had been laid for supper. Seven knifes and forks lay beside seven plates, on each of which had been placed a piece of bread. Seven glasses, each filled with wine, stood by each plate, and seven chairs were pulled up around the table, one for each of the places set. On the far side of the room were seven beds with seven neatly turned down counterpanes tucked in place.

She took a sip of wine from each of the glasses and broke a small piece of

bread from each plate. Then, her hunger and thirst satisfied, she lay down on one of the beds to sleep. She found the first bed far too small and moved to the next: this one was far too hard and so after trying all the rest she picked the one nearest to the wall in the far corner. In no time at all she was fast asleep.

Presently, while she slept, the seven masters of the cottage came in through the door. They entered one by one – seven small men with seven small caps – they were dwarfs. Each day they journeyed to the mountains to search for gold. One by one they each took a lantern from seven hooks and lit them, then they sat around the table to begin their supper.

"Wait a minute!" said the first. "Someone's been nibbling at my bread!"

"And mine too!" said the second.

"And drinking from my glass!" said the third.

"And from mine!" said the fourth.

"Who could it be?" asked the fifth.

"I can't begin to guess," said the sixth.

"I can! Look yonder, on my bed," it was the seventh dwarf who spoke.

Seven pairs of eyes swiveled toward the gloom of the far corner and saw the recumbent figure sleeping soundly. Stealthily, holding their lanterns high, they crept closer to investigate. The light from their candles revealed Snow White's peaceful slumbering face.

"Good heavens! What a beautiful child she is!"

"Ssh! Don't wake her."

"Do you think she's warm enough? We'd better cover her with a blanket."

The seven dwarfs tiptoed about, fussing with blankets and tucking her in snugly. Each was enchanted by her beauty and each was mindful not to wake her, creeping about as silently as a mouse. When at last they went to bed the seventh dwarf, whose bed Snow White had chosen, shared an hour in turn with each of his brothers.

When Snow White first awoke, she was surprised to find the seven little men sitting all around her bed, but then she saw their kind faces and concerned expressions and she was reassured. She told them her story and they shook their heads and tut-tutted at her words, murmuring disapprovingly whenever the queen was mentioned.

"There's nothing for it . . . you must stay here with us," said the first. "Should you care to cook and spin, and wash and sew for us, then we in turn will take good care of you." His six brothers thought it was a fine idea and immediately began to chatter all at the same time.

"Take care though," said the seventh, looking apprehensive and hushing his brothers. "This queen has an evil heart and she will soon discover where you are." He frowned and raised a finger to his lips: "When we are at our work, be warned! Let no one in lest you be carried away!" He wagged his finger importantly. The other six looked serious and were silent.

Now, far away the evil queen paced through her castle. The groom had told her Snow White was dead and a chill smile of triumph played about her lips. She went straight to her chamber and spoke to her magic mirror.

> *"Now, glass, I shall ask of thee,*
> *Who is the fairest? Is it me?"*

The mirror seemed for a moment to shimmer and the queen's reflection was distorted, then it replied.

> *"Thou, queen, art fairest here to see,*
> *But far away in the green wood's lea,*
> *Where seven dwarfs their home have made;*
> *There Snow White lives within the glade*
> *And she is lovelier far, than thee."*

The queen was outraged and screamed at the mirror. "You lie! You lie! It cannot be!" But in her heart she knew the mirror spoke the truth. She rushed from the room and swept down to the depths of the castle to seek out her maid. She seized the frightened girl and tore the simple robe from her back. Donning it herself the queen stormed into the castle yard; there, she rubbed mud into her face and hair to hide her beauty. Her frantic efforts were well rewarded – she had been transformed from a beautiful queen into a wretched-looking peasant woman. With her disguise complete, she set off to find Snow White in her hiding place – and when she did, she planned to destroy her.

Later the following day Snow White was busying herself in the little cottage when she heard a woman calling in a sing-song voice. "Cottons and cloth! Linen and lace! Fine wares, fine wares." The words drifted through the open window and Snow White paused in her work. At the window she saw the smiling face of a poor peddler woman. Truly, she looked quite wretched, but her manner seemed friendly and Snow White went to open the door.

"Good day, good woman," she said brightly. "And what do you sell today?" The woman bobbed and bowed, then she darted her grubby hand into a large wicker basket. "Why, my pretty one, laces and ribbons for a beauty such as yourself." She glanced down at Snow White's bodice as if surprised.

"My my, your laces are amiss, my dear! Let me give you a new one – fine and strong. Stand straight, my child, while I set you right."

Snow White did as she was told and the woman scuttled around behind her. Taking a silken cord from her basket the peddler woman busied herself with Snow White's laces. Suddenly, Snow White felt the cord slip around her throat, it tightened sharply driving the breath from her lungs. In seconds the woman had drawn the cord tight and firmly knotted it around Snow White's neck. Slowly Snow White slipped to the ground as if she were dead. The peasant woman hopped about the motionless figure, then with a last spiteful hiss at the stricken child, she vanished into the thick trees of the forest.

Some while later the dwarfs returned from their labors and found their beloved Snow White sprawled by their doorway. She appeared to be dead, but then the seventh dwarf noticed the silken cord around her throat – swiftly he drew his knife and severed it cleanly through.

The dwarfs carried her limp body into the cottage and laid her gently on her bed. They gathered round with much concern, patting and pampering; rubbing soothing oil into the vicious weal on her neck and warming her cold hands in theirs. At last she gave a deep sigh and her

eyes flickered open uncertainly. They were so relieved to see that she was still alive that a general chatter started up immediately.

"Hush now, brothers," it was the seventh dwarf. "Snow White has need of rest . . . she must sleep." Then he turned to the still shaken child and added: "From now on, no one must be allowed inside the cottage! No one! The peddler woman must surely have been the evil queen herself, intent to do you harm. Without question she will return when she discovers her wicked plan has failed."

Meanwhile the evil queen drew close to her castle; she paused by a tiny stream and washed away the grime of her disguise. Sweeping up to the castle gate she passed the astonished guards in her ragged clothes and went straight to her chamber to address the magic mirror. Its answer made the blood run cold in her veins.

"Where seven dwarfs their home have made,
There Snow White lives within the glade.
She still lives and breathes quite free
And is still lovelier far, than thee."

Shrieking with horror and fury at the mirror's words the queen took up a cane and struck at it again and again, but try as she might it did not shatter. Its magic was too powerful and instead of falling in splinters at her feet it merely repeated the terrible words.

The queen's anger knew no bounds, and turned within her, to a cold hatred that shrouded her heart with malice. "So! She still lives! I will devise a plan that guarantees her death. The next time I pay her a visit . . . will be the last!"

For three long days and three whole nights the queen was locked within her chamber. Every second of her time was spent pouring over her ancient books of magic and slowly she devised her wicked scheme.

When the third day had closed into darkness and the bats flitted from the creviced walls, the queen emerged from her room. No one in the world would have recognized her, so well had her magic worked. Gone was her fair skin and graceful form – in its place was a creature so misshapen as to put fear in the heart of the bravest man. Her nose and chin had become extended and stretched far beyond her sunken blubbery lips; her skin was yellow and drawn tight over her bony skull – it bristled like a hog's and was covered with ugly warts. A huge hump pressed down on her left shoulder and on the same side a withered hand, its long horny nails curling together like a bony cage, clutched at a gnarled stick. It was, however, her eyes that struck the deepest fear; they were sunk deep into their wrinkled sockets and were a deep blood-red, burning fiercely with the fires of hatred and revenge.

Down in the deepest dungeons of the castle the queen's grotesque form curled over a bubbling cauldron of vile smelling liquid. Beside it lay the dismembered remains of its deadly contents – it was a potion so poisonous that it could kill a thousand men. At last, mixed to her satisfaction, the queen took an apple from the castle kitchen. She pierced its rosy skin with a needle and injected a measure of the evil liquid. She had taken great care to choose the most delicious-looking apple; it glistened with tempting crispness yet, beyond the tiny pinprick, it betrayed no sign of its deadly power. The queen placed it in a basket, with others that were untainted, then she set out for the forest . . . and Snow White's cottage.

Once again, Snow White was disturbed at her work in the tiny cottage, but this time she was truly alarmed at the stranger's hideous appearance.

"What is it you want?" she asked the old woman nervously.

"Only to sell my fine fresh fruit, my dear," said the old crone. "Open your door and let me in."

Snow White remembered the dwarf's words of warning and answered quickly: "I dare not. I am bade to keep the door locked and not let anyone in."

A hollow gurgle echoed up from the old hag's throat and she shrugged her twisted shoulders awkwardly, the great hump rocking back and forth. "As you please, my pretty miss, but take this rosy apple – let it be a present from me to you." And she passed the poisoned fruit through the open window.

Snow White recoiled in horror as the withered claw stretched towards her. "No, I cannot! I dare not!" she exclaimed.

The claw rotated the apple back and forth mechanically as if to show how fresh and fine it was. "Why, you silly girl. Do you think that it is poison? Come, I'll eat the same to prove that it is sound."

The hag placed the poisoned apple on the window sill where the sun glinted on its rosy skin. Snow White was sorely tempted to reach for the enticing fruit – it looked so fresh and inviting. She watched intently as the old woman bit deeply into another juicy apple taken from her basket. Her bloated jaws chomped noisily up and down and Snow White could no longer resist the temptation – she reached out and picked up the poisoned apple. She could smell its crisp freshness as she raised it to her lips and she took just one small bite. Instantly, her eyes flickered shut and she fell lifeless to the ground.

That night the queen spoke again to her magic mirror and it uttered the words that filled her envious heart with triumphant joy.

"Thou, queen, art fairest of them all."

The seven dwarfs found the body of Snow White when they returned from work. She was truly dead and their sorrow was immeasurable. They lifted her crumpled form and carried it tenderly to her bed. They lovingly combed her long black hair and washed her grimy brow; they touched a drop of wine to her lips, but their efforts were in vain – no sigh came from between her cherry-red lips, no heart beat within her breast.

The dwarfs were moved to tears in their grief: for seven days they sat beside her stricken form and quietly mourned her passing – not one departed from his vigil to go to the mountains; not one took bread or wine, and each day at least one was seen to shed a tear.

At length it was proposed that they should bury her – it should be within the forest where the bluebells grew at their thickest. But then they looked upon her snow-white skin and it was as pure as ever – as if she were still alive: her cheeks remained rosy red and her ebony hair cascaded over her breast and shone like a raven's wing.

The dwarfs could not bear to face a single day without a sight of her fair beauty, so between them they made a crystal coffin and lined it with silken cushions. There, they gently laid her and she rested as if asleep. On the lid they wrote her name in golden letters, and beneath it added that she was the daughter of a king.

The casket was taken to a nearby hilltop and not a single day passed without one of the faithful dwarfs sitting close beside her. The creatures of

the forest came to pay their respects and stood close by – the wolf and the fawn together, like enemies at truce, united in their grief. The birds of the air flew down and gilded the casket with fallen autumn leaves and brightly colored feathers. An owl glided silently by and paused to mourn a while; a raven, burnished black, flapped sadly at her feet and lastly, a dove with a snow-white breast swooped and cooed a last lament.

Thus she lay for a long time – as though still sleeping and yet unchanged.

It was just so when a prince passed by one day. He noted the sun glinting from an object on the hilltop and guided his horse to its source – there he found the crystal casket and close by a dwarf was sitting quietly.

He saw Snow White upon her bed of silken cushions and his heart was filled with love for her. She was so beautiful that he couldn't take his eyes from her peaceful sleeping face. He spoke to the dwarf, asking if he might carry her away to his palace: there he would set her on a golden bier where he could gaze upon her beauty every day.

The dwarf shook his head and his brothers gathered round. "We will not part with her for all the riches of the world."

They circled the casket and folded their arms defiantly.

The prince smiled and spoke kindly to them. "Good sirs, I mean to take nothing from you – nor would I despoil her rest, but her beauty has truly captured my heart. Pray, let me then just press my lips upon her crystal counterpane."

The dwarfs mumbled among themselves and, nodding silently, stepped aside. The prince approached and bent low over the sleeping figure. His lips were on the point of kissing the chill crystal when he accidentally jogged the casket with his arm. The casket trembled and the sparkling lights that danced on its surface shivered. Inside, the tiny piece of poisoned apple fell from Snow White's lips and she opened her eyes. "Where am I?" she whispered.

Later she learned from the dwarfs what had happened since she had fallen asleep. The handsome prince asked that she be his wife and Snow White consented to his wish. Together with the dwarfs they set out for the prince's palace to make preparations for their wedding.

All the people of the land were invited to the wedding feast; the nobles and the squires and the kings and queens from the neighboring kingdoms: among these last was the evil queen herself. She was now grown old but each day still, she asked her magic mirror the same question. Since the day she had poisoned Snow White she had received the same answer, but on the day of the wedding the mirror gave her a different reply.

> *"Your beauty once was fairest, queen,*
> *But now tis gone, for that I've seen.*
> *So go and seek out far away*
> *The fairest – Snow White weds today!"*

The queen's wrinkled face creased with frustrated anger, although she did not want to believe that Snow White was still alive after so long a time, her curiosity and envy drove her to accept the invitation to the wedding and she determined to see the girl again.

Her heart pounded as she rushed to the prince's palace in her carriage; it pounded harder as she flew up the steps and entered the great hall; and pounded still more as she pushed her way through the throng of guests gathered around the happy couple. Then, before her, stood Snow White – as fair and beautiful as ever and not looking a day older.

The pounding in the evil queen's breast felt like a wild beast tearing at her soul. She clutched wildly at her throat and tried to speak, but the pounding grew louder in her ears and a strangled cry erupted from her twisted lips. Her eyes rolled and she reached out towards Snow White, clutching at the air, but then she fell with a gasp to the floor. The pounding in her cruel heart was stilled forever and she lay dead at Snow White's feet.

Snow White and her prince lived on for many years and were happy together in their palace. Each night they dined in the great hall and always there were nine places set at table – one for Snow White and one for the prince, and seven for her faithful friends – the seven dwarfs.

The Robber Groom

HERE ONCE LIVED A MILLER who had the prettiest daughter a man could wish for. She was fair of face and form, and delightful in her manner to all who knew her.

As time went by she grew from a pretty child into a beautiful young woman. "It is time," thought the miller, "for her to marry. I shall seek a suitable groom to welcome as a son. When I find a man I can trust I will give him my daughter's hand in marriage."

The miller gave a great deal of thought to this affair and whenever he went to the market, he would talk with his many friends and ask them about their sons. A suitable match would soon be found.

Now the miller was very rich from grinding the corn gathered from miles about. His daughter, when she married, would therefore have a rich dowry: she would be a prize for a less-than-honest man. The miller was also shrewd and although he didn't care whether his daughter's groom was rich or poor, he must on all accounts be honest and true and love her for herself alone.

News of the miller's wealth and of his beautiful daughter spread far and wide and many would-be suitors came to visit the mill. The wily miller saw that most were merely after his daughter's dowry and sent them off with a flea in their ear.

One day the miller heard a knock at the door and when he opened it found a handsome stranger standing there. His clothes showed him to be a man of some wealth and his horse was well-harnessed with the finest tack.

The young man rested with them for the evening and talked quite charmingly of this and that, admiring the miller's house and assuring him of his reputation as the finest miller throughout the land. The miller was soon won over and encouraged the young man's attentions to his

daughter. She, as always, was politely mannered, but behind her smile she nursed a secret doubt about the stranger.

Within a week the young man asked the miller for his daughter's hand in marriage. The miller readily agreed and was delighted at having found so perfect a match for his daughter: not only did the young man possess good looks and money of his own, but by all accounts, had a fine house and estate where his daughter could live quite comfortably. Indeed, the miller thought, his motives were beyond reproach.

The miller's daughter abided by her father's wishes and consented to

the marriage, but deep within her heart she felt no love for the young man. He visited her daily and paid her compliments, yet although she measured his charm she would shudder at his touch and his silken tongue sent a creeping chill into her very bones.

One day he declared that since she was to be his wife, she should visit his house to see where she would live after the wedding. Flustered, she answered that she didn't know where his house was.

"But it's quite near," he chided. "In yonder forest, set among the tallest trees."

Still she did not visit, pretending she did not know the way.

"Tomorrow you *will* come to my house." The young man had grown quite insistent. "I will lay a trail for you to follow through the forest. I will scatter ashes along the path and you will easily find your way." The miller's daughter searched her mind for an excuse but he went on: "Besides, I have invited friends to meet you and I know they will be sorely offended if you do not come." His words got the better of her good nature and for the sake of his friends, she agreed.

When morning came her mind was troubled; something sinister about the young man's manner made her wary, even fearful. So, just before she set out, she filled her pockets with peas and beans. Then, as she traced the scattered ashes through the forest, she dropped a bean to the left and a pea to the right with every step.

It was late in the afternoon and the shadows had grown long when she came at last to a dark house hunched amidst the tall, overhanging trees. It appeared to be deserted and was cold and foreboding. The stillness of

the forest thereabouts sent a shiver down her spine as she stealthily approached. She reached the crumbling stone steps that led up to the dark sunken doorway and was about to ascend when she was startled by a shrill cry:

> *"Turn again, my bonny bride,*
> *Return to your safe home.*
> *Haste from the robber's den and hide*
> *Let it not be your tomb."*

Above her head she saw a wicker cage hanging from the portal. Inside a robin hopped about and flapped its wings. She took a further step towards the door.

> *"Turn again, my bonny bride,*
> *Return to your safe home.*
> *Haste from the robber's den and hide*
> *Let it not be your tomb."*

She smiled at the robin's antics but paid no heed to its repeated warning. She climbed the steps and entered the house; inside it was dark and gloomy and as silent as the grave. She picked her way from room to room but all were empty, there was no sign of her intended groom or of his guests. She climbed the stairs but again found all the rooms were deserted. At last, set high beneath the roof in the attic, she came upon a narrow doorway. She went in and found an old woman sitting close to a small window slanting down from the roof. She appeared to be asleep but then the girl saw that her eyes were gazing out across the treetops into the far distance.

"I beg your pardon, good lady," said the miller's daughter. "But pray tell me if this is the house of my intended husband?"

The old woman clasped her gnarled old hands together tightly and a shadow of fear flickered across her face.

"Ah, my child, so you have fallen into his trap." Her voice was kind and she leaned forward in her chair. Her eyes widened as she spoke again: "You have come here to be the bride of Death!" Her voice was barely a whisper. "Your fine young man is a common robber. His fine clothes and horse belong to long-dead travelers. Now, he means to steal your greatest gift . . . your life!"

The old woman rose from her chair and her bones creaked and groaned. "He will return soon for his supper. I must hide you or your life is lost." She took hold of the girl's hand. "Come, be quick!"

She led the girl to a great hall and hid her behind a pile of huge wine casks. "Do not stir, my child, be as quiet as a mouse. When the robbers sleep we will escape." The old woman paused and then she added quietly: "Will you take me with you? I have long wanted to leave this wretched place, but my eyes are dim and my years bade me stay. With you to guide me I too can be free."

"Of course," said the girl and she kissed the old woman's wrinkled cheek. Outside they heard the sound of horses' hooves approaching. The old woman just had time to push the barrels close about the girl when the robbers entered the room.

From her hiding place the miller's daughter heard their rough voices and recognized among them that of her would-be husband; it was coarse and no longer carried its silken tones. She also heard the terrified cries of a young girl, made captive by the evil band. She listened to them drink and feast and heard the poor maid's pleas for mercy. She heard them force the wine to the maid's lips and heard her gasp as she fell dead.

The miller's daughter trembled for fear that they would discover her hiding place and kill her too. Her heart was beating so loudly she felt sure they would hear its pounding. She crouched lower but then a voice spoke out above the rest.

"Be still, you rogues!" It was the robber-groom. "Now that this wretch is dead, I'll have the gold from her finger." He snatched at the ring but it flew from his hands across the room. The miller's daughter heard it rolling, rolling . . . towards her hiding place. Then the ring was at her feet, tumbling still, and gleaming dully in the flickering candlelight. She snatched it up and held her breath.

"The Devil! Where's it gone?" The curse was followed by the robber's heavy steps and she heard the first rasp of a barrel being heaved to one side.

"Leave it for now!" It was the old woman's voice. "Come to your food. It's late and rabbit pie is best when hot. The ring will still be there tomorrow, it'll not run away, I'll be bound."

So the robbers gave up their search and went on with their eating and their drinking. The miller's daughter let out a long sigh and waited.

Meanwhile, the old woman had mixed a powerful sleeping draught –

when the robbers were not looking she slipped it into the jug of wine. Soon, the robbers were snoring loudly. They sprawled across the scattered plates and spilt wine on the long table and lay crumpled on the floor where they had fallen in their drunken stupor.

The girl crept from behind the barrels and picked her way fearfully towards the door. One of the robbers growled noisily in his sleep as she passed and her heart missed a beat. In the corner of the room she saw the crumpled figure of their murdered victim and her eyes filled with tears.

At last she was out of the dreadful room and, taking the old woman's arm, she left the house and its murderous occupants.

The moon was high and the forest was bathed in silver light as the two threaded their way through the trees. Rain had fallen and the ashes had been washed away, but in their place they found the young shoots of peas and beans sprouting up on either side of the path. They walked, all through the night, for the old woman moved slowly, and it was dawn when they finally reached the mill.

The miller was beside himself with rage when he heard his daughter's tale. He sat down in his chair for a long time to calm down, and at length, a cold thoughtful look came into his eyes.

"You may stay with us as our guest . . . as long as you wish." He told the old woman. Then he turned to his daughter and whispered his plan. "The wedding will take place, my dear." But she thought she detected a chuckle in his voice as he took her in his arms.

The day of the wedding arrived. The miller invited all his friends and relations. He had also sent word to the robber-groom to be certain to bring his friends as well. Sure enough, the brigands rode up and sat themselves down at the wedding table to enjoy the feast.

When all had had their fill the miller proposed that each and every guest should tell a tale to entertain their fellows. It was soon a merry gathering as tale followed tale, but then at last it came to the turn of the miller's daughter.

"Come now, my dear," sneered the robber-groom. "Have you no tongue? Do you have a tale to tell us?"

She answered lightly: "Yes, but it is but a dream I had, my dear."

The guests leaned forward to listen to her tale.

"I dreamed of a wood, and a lonely house – and a robin who spoke of my death. I dreamed of an old woman who hid me behind a cask of wine to save me from a robber band. She bade me be still and quiet as a mouse." The guests were open-mouthed and waited on her every word.

"I dreamed the robbers came, and with them brought a captive maid. I dreamed they forced the poison wine between her lips and I dreamed she fell dead at their feet. I dreamed a robber snatched at her finger to tear off her golden ring, and I dreamed it rolled away and settled at my feet."

A stunned silence had come upon the gathering, broken only by the sound of the robbers nervously shuffling their feet.

"And then, my child, what next did you dream?" It was the old woman who had crept from the mill and was now standing right behind the robber-groom. He was shaken by the sound of her voice that he knew so well, but he was rooted to his seat with fear.

"Then, good mother, I picked it up . . . and here it is!"

The robber looked with disbelief at the ring and his face went as white as snow; his eyes blinked wildly and he made to rise from the table. But, to his dismay, he was unable to flee: the miller had chosen his guests with care and strong arms pinned the robber to his seat. Others held his companions down and at length they were taken off to justice.

And the miller's daughter? Aye, she married a fine young man. His strong arms first caught her eye at the wedding feast. Now, she is happy with children of her own. Her husband is honest and true and works the mill. While the old miller – he sits in the sun and smiles at his grandchildren and tells them tales of long ago, of fair maidens and robbers – and clever millers.

Tom Thumb

IN A WET LAND, FLAT LAND, farther-away-than-that land lived a farmer and his wife. Every evening they would sit by the fire and talk of do's and don'ts and will's and won'ts: nothing special, but often they would laugh. Sometimes they couldn't even remember what it was they laughed at – but it was always funny. One thing they often talked about was how much work they had to do – and who was to do it?

Sometimes when they had laughed a lot and the evening drew on, they would grow sleepy; then they would become a little sad and talk of children. They had none of their own and this made them feel lonely.

"Oh, if only I had a son of my own. He could keep me company in the fields," said the farmer. "If I had but one wish, it would be for a son – even a little one," and the old man chuckled softly to himself at the thought.

"If I had a son to love and to hug then I'd not be lonely when you're out working, m'dear." The old woman warmed her hands in front of the fire. Holding one up she said: "Just as big as this thumb, he need be no bigger!" Once more they broke into a merry chuckle and rocked back in their comfy chairs.

Surely it must have been the night when wishes were granted for the following morning a very strange thing happened. The farmer had gone out to the fields and his wife was about to make some bread. She took down her great jar of flour; then some salt and a little yeast, and then a big jug of water. She started to mix and knead, knead and mix; suddenly, the pastry in her hands went "POP!"

"Hello mother!" said a cheery voice. There, on the kitchen table and covered in flour from top to toe, stood a tiny boy – no bigger than the old woman's thumb!

"Well I never!" she said and her shoulders bobbed up and down as she

chuckled at the little lad's antics. He was dancing about on the table amid a cloud of flour.

"Well I never!" said the astonished farmer when he came home for lunch.

"Hello father, can I come with you this afternoon and help in the fields?" said the tiny figure.

"Well, my little Tom Thumb, of course you can. But I've got to take out the big cart to collect up all the beets I've dug. It's very high and I doubt you're tall enough to help me load it."

"But that's no problem. I'll drive the cart while you load it with beets." And Tom clapped his tiny hands together as the matter was settled.

"All you need do," he went on, "is place me behind the horse's ear and I'll guide him along beside you."

The farmer chuckled and chortled and his good wife laughed.

That afternoon the farmer stooped and heaved the piles of fresh-dug beets into the back of the cart. Each time he moved to the next pile, a small voice called out: "Giddyup! Move along there!" The horse would prick up his ears and take a few paces more to keep up with the farmer.

Nearby, two rascals watched with open mouths. A horse that moved and pulled a cart without a driver? Whatever next!

"Giddyup! Move along there!" And again the horse moved on.

"A horse that walks and *talks*?" One rascal croaked.

"Indeed, a speciality," said the other. "I think it's worth a second look." The first rascal stepped forward right on to the toes of the second rascal and they fell in a tangled heap amid the muddy beets. Clumsily they struggled to their feet and went towards the farmer.

"Now if we smile, we'll hide our guile."

The farmer watched the two rascals draw near but stooping low he tended to his work.

"Good day, kind sir. My, what a horse! To guide itself without recourse . . . no driver or what else, heh! heh!" The rascals smirked and held their arms. The farmer winced at their false charms.

"No, 'tis just my son," was the farmer's reply, eyeing them slowly and turning to the horse that stood patiently waiting beside him. He lifted Tom down from behind the horse's ear. "He may be small but he is help enough to me."

"Well, I'll be . . ." The rascal nearest fell back against his fellow and, lying on his back in the mud, became the rascal furthest.

The other spoke: "I see," his voice was low and wheedling, "and may I

ask what price he'd fetch? I see a trade with such as he, and useful too, alongside me." He smiled craftily at the farmer. "What'll it be, my fine fellow, gold or gilders? They're both yellow!" A croaky chuckle gurgled from the villain's throat.

"Tom's not for sale. He's my own flesh and blood. I'll not sell my son, nor take your gold!" The farmer took a step backwards and folded his arms across his chest. Meanwhile, Tom had crept up to his father's shoulder and he whispered in his ear behind a cupped hand: "Go on, father, let them make you rich. Take their gold; I'll soon be back, you'll see."

The farmer nodded slowly and the gold changed hands.

Now Tom astride the villain's hat wobbled along above their chat.

"He'll make our fortune, you'll see. We'll sneak him in to turn the key."

"Then rich mens' gold and jewels we'll take. Enough for life . . . a tidy stake."

All the while Tom listened but then the two of them sniggered and tripped and down they went again into the mud. Tom flew off the rascal's hat and landed nimbly on a tuft of grass. "What now, my lords, are we to tumble all day long? Or is there work for me to do?"

The rascals leered and both bent close.

"It's very simple Tom, m'lad. I seem to have mislaid my key. That's where you come in, d'you see?"

"Yes, quiet like, and let us in. Don't wake no one, don't make a din."

Tom nodded his head pleasantly but saw through the villains' scheme. They meant to rob and steal; and to use him to help them do it. Tom was thoughtful but inside his head his brain was buzzing – he made a plan to foil their ruse.

That night the two rascals crept up to the squire's house – he was the richest man for miles about. Carefully they set Tom on the window sill and bade him crawl through between the bars to open the door. Tom clambered through and slipped down to the floor within. Then, when he had straightened himself up he turned back to the window and shouted as loud as he could: "I'll not be long, just you wait there!"

"Ssh . . . not so loud!" hissed the villains from the window and they jostled against each other in their efforts to squeeze closer to the bars.

"What's that you say?" yelled Tom. "I can't quite hear you!" His lungs were fit to burst and his tiny voice was so loud that it woke up the cook and the groom, who woke up the maid, who woke up the butler, who woke up the squire . . . and his wife.

"Stay by the window while I open the door!" shrieked Tom even louder. Suddenly the door opened, but it wasn't Tom who appeared.

"There by the window! See! Where? Over there!" First came the cook with a rolling-pin; next came the maid with a broom; then came the butler with a pained expression; then came the groom with a sharpened stick – and last came the squire . . . and his wife.

The two villains were so surprised that they took off across the fields like frightened rabbits, tumbling and stumbling over one another in their haste to escape.

Later, when the rascals were safely behind bars in the local jail, and the house was quiet again, Tom came out of his hiding place. He had been laughing so much he feared he'd be discovered, but no one had bothered to look inside the coffeepot! He left the house and ran into the moonlit yard, seeing a large barn he entered it and lay down on a pile of warm straw to sleep away the rest of the night.

Alas for Tom, before he woke, the grumbly groom came to the barn to feed the cows and scooped up the straw wherein lay Tom. It wasn't until Tom stretched himself awake that he found he was already inside a cow's mouth. The large brown cow munched and munched and Tom was about to be swallowed!

"Oh my! What have I got myself into!" Tom exclaimed as he tumbled down into the cow's stomach. A great deal of straw was tumbling in after him and soon Tom felt quite squeezed inside the cow.

"No more, no more, there's no more room!" he cried. But unknown to Tom, the milkmaid had just begun to milk the cow he was in. The sound of Tom's voice was too much for her and she fell off her three-legged stool and upset her pail of milk.

"No more, no more, there's no more room in here!"

There it was again. The milkmaid screamed and ran to tell the squire.

"Nonsense, my dear. Cows do not talk," he said sternly.

"But sir, please sir, beg your pardon sir, it's not only talking, it's shouting at me!"

The squire decided to see for himself; so along went his wife, the butler and the cook, the groom and the maid – into the barn. They stopped and stared: there stood the docile warm-eyed cow contentedly chewing away.

"No more straw, I tell you! I'm getting squashed in here!"

"I don't believe it," said the squire and neither did his wife.

"'Tis true then," said the cook, and the parlor maid said "Yes!"

"Tut, tut," said the butler and looked the other way.

"Best to 'ave 'er butchered," said the bad-tempered groom. But the cow nuzzled into a fresh pile of straw and went on munching.

"She must be sick," said the squire. "Quite right," agreed his wife.

"Send for the farmer who lives across the field," and the groom trudged out as the squire had declared.

Within an hour the farmer who, would you believe, was Tom's father, arrived at the barn. He looked at the cow and listened to the tiny voice calling from inside it. He cocked his head to one side and then gave it a thoughtful scratch. "Well now, my lord, 'tis not much to fret about. I'll soon have her right." Then, chuckling quietly to himself, he added in a whisper: "My word, whatever will my Tom get into next?"

He sent for a bucket of warm water and took from his pocket an assortment of tiny bottles. One by one he emptied their contents into the bucket – first green liquid, and then red liquid, then blue liquid and finally orange liquid. The mixture was stirred.

At last, after a lot of stirring, the farmer reached for a large spoon.

Filling it from the bucket he whispered in the cow's ear and emptied the mixture down the beast's throat.

A few moments passed and the whole gathering drew close about the cow. The cow stopped chewing and stood very still. A strange faraway look came into her eye and a faint rumbling sound came from deep within her belly. It was clear that the mixture was beginning to have an effect and the ladies were ushered out of the barn. It was not a moment too soon either. Hardly had they left when the cow lifted its tail high in the air, gave a long low moan and "Splat!" There was Tom sitting on the floor of the barn in a most ungracious state!

The farmer shoveled Tom into a bucket while all about held their noses. Then he loaded the bucket onto the back of his cart and drove home, taking the cart right up to the pump in his back yard.

"My word!" chuckled Tom's mother. "You are in a terrible mess, my lad." She pushed Tom under the streaming pump while his father chugged the long handle up and down. She took off Tom's smelly clothes and dumped him in a bathful of suds. She scrubbed and scrubbed until her little lad was pink all over and as clean as ever he had been.

"There now, my lad, that's better," she said and wrapped him in a large white towel before the fire to dry.

"You have had a fine old day," said his father kindly. "And did you find your adventures exciting, Tom?"

"Yes father," said Tom quietly. "I've been out to see the world, but I must say it's easy to get into trouble, isn't it?"

The farmer looked fondly at his tiny son . . . "Such a little adventurer," he thought. "It's as well I've got a way with cows, Tom."

Hansel and Gretel

O N THE TABLE lay one small piece of bread: it was all there was to feed three people – a poor woodsman, his wife and their son Hansel. Once, the woodman had been able to make a good living by cutting and selling logs, but now he had fallen on hard times and had no money whatsoever.

"It's no good just sitting there," snapped his wife crossly. "You'll just have to go and cut more logs. More wood to sell will mean more money to buy food! We can't go on like this, you know, we need to fill our bellies!"

On and on she nagged at her miserable husband. "And this boy of ours! He is getting bigger every day! Only seven years old? He eats enough for ten men!"

The woodsman couldn't bear to listen to his wife's ranting any longer and picking up his axe he left the cottage and went to the woods. After the noisy anger within his home, the woodsman found the silent trees around him cool and peaceful; he began to feel quite cheerful. "I will cut more wood today than ever before," he said to himself as he swung along the forest track. Presently, at his feet, he came upon what appeared to be a bundle of rags. He bent to take a closer look and the rags moved beneath his hand. Somewhat startled, he drew back in surprise, and saw that the bundle was a sleeping child.

"Why, my little love," he whispered. "What are you doing here all alone?" The woodsman brushed her golden hair from her brow and as he did so, she opened her eyes – they were the deepest blue he'd ever seen. She looked up into his kind face and told him her story.

She could remember sitting behind her father on his horse; she could remember feeling sleepy, then there had been a bump and she had found herself sitting on the forest track. She told him how she'd run off in search of her father, but it had grown dark and she had crept into a thicket and fallen asleep.

The woodsman was thoughtful: the poor child must have run off the
wrong way. Her father probably searched for her but in the gloom of
dusk had not seen her sleeping beside the track.

"Well now, you must come home with me," he said. "Are you
hungry?" He took her hand and started back towards his home.

"Yes, I suppose I am," said the little girl brightly and she skipped
along beside him and appeared none the worse for her adventure.

"It's not too far to walk, little one," said the woodsman and then he
asked her name.

"My name is Gretel . . . and I'm six years old."

The woodsman laughed. "Well, you'll be a fine playmate for my
young son. He's just a mite older than you, but just as bright, I'll
warrant." On the way back to his cottage he caught a rabbit in one of his
snares. His wife would be pleased, he thought, at least they'd have a fine

supper that night, it would be a pleasant change.

Later, after they had eaten and the two children were tucked up in their beds, the woodsman's wife began to scold him again.

"Yes, a fine supper indeed! But you've cut no wood at all today and we've now an extra mouth to feed! Have you no sense?" Her words saddened him and he sunk deeper into his old chair and remained silent. He was, without question, a very poor man and his nagging wife was right – where, indeed, would he find enough food for an extra mouth?

Time passed and Hansel and Gretel grew to love each other like brother and sister but their father's misfortunes grew worse. Not only were there fewer people to buy his logs, but he had also badly chipped the blade of his axe on a fallen tree and had no money to buy a new one.

At night he tossed and turned on his bed with worry. His wife beside him hushed and grumbled and at last turned on him angrily: "Husband, do as others do! The girl was found by you so let her be found again by someone else! Take her back to the wood, and Hansel too! That way, at least, they will be fed by richer folk than us."

The woodsman was distressed and answered her quickly. "No, I cannot do that – abandon them without a care?"

"Well husband, if you do not, we will starve. You'll see!"

They argued back and forth until, in despair, the woodsman agreed to her plan – he would do as she suggested.

Meanwhile, their raised voices had woken the two children. They had heard the woman's hard words and her plan had disturbed them greatly, causing them to cling together for comfort. At length the woodsman and his wife were silent and all that could be heard was the steady snoring of the sleeping couple. It was then that Hansel tiptoed to the door and looked outside. The moon was shining brightly and the pebbles scattered about the yard gleamed like silver coins in the cold light. Hansel gathered as many as he could and filled his pockets to the brim before returning to his bed. "Don't worry, sister," he told Gretel. "I will keep us safe."

The next morning the woman tugged them roughly awake and bundled them into their clothes. "We're going to the woods today," she snapped. "Now, hurry up! I've not got time to waste on you two."

They set off, and as they walked, Hansel let the pebbles drop, one by one, along the path between the trees. Soon they stopped and the woodsman made a fire. "Stay here, my loves," his voice was sad, "while

we gather berries and search for wild mushrooms. Be sure to wait until we return.'' His wife snorted crossly and frowned at them without a word, then she turned her back and tramped off through the bushes behind her sorrowful husband.

The children waited and waited and listened – the sound of their parents' shuffling in the woods grew fainter and fainter. Soon all they could hear was the chirping of birds in the trees. As dusk fell, even they became silent, and Gretel began to cry. Hansel put his arm about her shoulder and threw some more twigs on the fire. "Don't cry, Gretel, we only have to wait for the moon to come out.''

It wasn't long before it did, and slipping from behind a cloud it shed its silvery glow over the forest. They looked between the trees and saw the trail of pebbles, glittering like tiny stars fallen to earth.

They followed the pebbles through the night and it was close to dawn when they knocked on the door of their home. The woodsman hugged them and flung his arms about them; his heart had been heavy from the moment he'd left them in the forest and now it was filled with joy. His wife, however, smiled coldly and pretended to be pleased: inside she was secretly angry that her plan had failed.

Once again the family grew tired and weak from lack of food, and once again the woman nagged her husband. "You must take them into the forest again, but this time to the deepest part. Then they will never be able to find their way out!'' Her voice was harsh in his ears. "Otherwise,'' she added, "we will surely starve to death!''

Once more Hansel heard his mother's cruel scheme and as before he tiptoed to the door to fetch some pebbles, but his mother had locked it and he couldn't get out.

When morning came their father gave them each a small piece of bread. He looked sternly at his wife then led the children into the forest.

"Keep hold of your piece of bread," whispered Hansel. "I will make sure we find our way home again." He crumbled the bread in his pocket and just as he had done with the pebbles, he let the crumbs fall beside the track as they walked along.

They went farther into the wood than they had ever been before and when they stopped their father again lit a fire. He quickly left them and told them to wait for his return. A long time passed – they began to feel hungry and so they shared Gretel's bread.

"When the moon rises we will see the crumbs I have dropped by the path," said Hansel. "They will guide us to our home."

Alas, when the moon came up there was no sign of the breadcrumbs – the birds of the forest had picked them all up and eaten them. Try as they might, the children could not find the path leading home, and they wandered deeper and deeper into the dark forest. They ate some berries but they were not enough to fill their bellies and finally, tired and exhausted, they crept into a hollow tree to sleep.

Three days passed by as they wandered amongst the trees, but on the third morning they were woken by the sound of the sweetest singing. It came from above them and looking up, they saw a snow-white bird perched on a branch. It fluttered and sang and hopped away from them; then it turned as if to say "Follow me, follow me!" The children ran toward it but again it fluttered away only to turn and wait for them. They followed the bird until, at last, it came to rest on the roof of a strange little house set deep amongst the trees. To their amazement they saw that the house was made of gingerbread with a roof of cake and windows of sugar.

"At last we have enough to eat," cried Hansel, running forward and breaking off a piece of the roof. "Try the sweet windows, sister, they will ease your hunger, I'll warrant."

But as the children gobbled away at the little house they suddenly heard a voice call out to them from within.

"Nibble, nibble, like a mouse.
Who is nibbling at my house?"

And they answered.

> *"Just the wind that blows free,*
> *Nothing else to bother thee."*

They continued to munch away, picking at the window-panes and tearing off lumps of cake from the roof and gingerbread from the walls. All at once the door flew open and out hopped a crooked little woman with a long crooked stick clutched in her crooked old hand. Hansel and Gretel were so startled that they dropped the cake and gingerbread they were eating and stood there with their eyes wide open. The old lady chuckled and bobbed her head up and down.

"Well well, my dears, and what brings you to my house? Come in, come in! There's no need to be alarmed – I will take care of you." This last was followed by a strange deep gurgle from way down in her throat. She took hold of their hands and led them inside the house. There, she brought out more food for them to eat – sweet pancakes and nuts, apples and honey, and jugs of milk. When they had eaten their fill, she made up two little beds with clean linen and bade them climb in to sleep. Hansel and Gretel were delighted and snuggled down happily as if they were in heaven. Within minutes both were sound asleep.

However, the old woman's kindness was false, her friendly manner a deception. She was a wicked witch with awesome powers and the senses of the wild beasts of the forest. The arrival of the two children had been no surprise to her; she had sensed their approach with her keen sense of smell when they were still far away. Her sharp ears had heard every sound they made as they crept through the forest and her magic had been put to use while she waited for them. Her gingerbread house was merely a trap set to entice the hungry children. Once caught, and in her power, she planned to eat them up.

The witch hovered low over the sleeping children and cackled softly to herself. "My, how pretty they are – and what a tasty dish they'll make!" Then as the first light of dawn crept over the window sill, she snatched Hansel up from his bed and threw him into a wicker cage behind the cottage. He began to cry but the witch shut down the barred door and locked it tightly. "There you'll stay, my little beauty, until you're fat enough to suit my taste!"

Next, she woke Gretel and shook her roughly by the shoulder. "Wake up you lazy child! Fetch some water to boil and cook up something good to eat. Your brother needs a deal of fattening before he's fit for my plate!"

Gretel was so distressed she too began to cry but it was to no avail and she was forced to do the old hag's bidding. Each day she worked and worked from morn till night, and the old witch scolded her all the time. She would cackle about and visit Hansel in his cage, asking that he poke out a finger. "Are you fat enough yet, my dear?" But her wicked eyes were dim and Hansel, seeking to deceive her, would poke out a spindly piece of bone through the bars of his cage. The witch would grunt impatiently and stomp away to wait another day.

The days stretched into weeks and finally the witch could wait no

longer. "'Tis time enough!" she hissed. "I'll cook him up with fat or not, but first I'll bake some bread to go with my meal."

In the corner of the cottage stood her great domed bread oven and the old crone stoked it up until it glowed red hot. Then she dragged Gretel towards it and opened up the iron door.

"Here, my pretty, hop inside and tell me if it's hot enough to brown my bread."

But Gretel saw the witch's purpose and pretended not to know how to climb inside the oven. Whereupon the old witch laughed scornfully and pushed the girl aside. "It's big enough to take a horse!" she cursed. "Here, I'll show you." She bent her crooked back and poked her wrinkled head low down to the open oven door. In one swift movement Gretel seized her chance and gave the witch a mighty shove from behind. The crone pitched forward headlong into the blazing oven and Gretel slammed the iron door shut.

While the wicked witch was baked alive, Gretel ran to open the door of Hansel's cage. He was free at last and the children hugged and kissed each other joyfully. Now that the witch was dead they were no longer fearful and they went about the cottage emptying drawers and tipping up boxes and bags all over the place. To their delight they found a treasure of pearls and jewels and a great hoard of gold and silver coins. These the witch had stolen from poor unfortunate travelers who had passed her way and fallen into her trap.

Quickly, the children filled their pockets to bursting with the treasure and ran towards the cottage door. There, Gretel paused and snatched up the witch's magic wand. "I'll take this too," she said. "It will be of help, for we have far to go from this dreadful place."

Their journey took them through the forest for many days. Often they found their path was blocked by the thickest briars or great fallen trees. Gretel would wave the magic wand and the path would clear before them. At last the trees began to grow thinner and they climbed to the top of a steep ridge overlooking a wide sweeping valley. From the top, the children looked down and far in the distance saw a thin curl of smoke, winding high into the cool morning air. It came from the chimney of a tiny woodsman's cottage – it was their home!

They scrambled down the grassy slope, laughing and tumbling, and calling out happily to each other, but when they reached the bottom they discovered a deep river; it had been hidden from them by a wall of drooping willow trees. The water was dark and wide with tendrils of green weed waving gently far down in the depths. There was no way they could cross and they sat sadly on the mossy bank looking across to the other side.

Then Gretel's face broke into a happy smile – she had suddenly remembered the magic wand. "I know," she said. "I will turn you, dear brother, into a swan and you can take me safely across on your broad back." Gretel pointed the wand at Hansel and waved it around him in a wide circle – instantly he was transformed into a great snow-white swan. Quickly she clambered on to the swan's broad back and he swam strongly over the dark waters of the wide river. When they reached the opposite side the swan waddled up through the thick reeds and Gretel waved her magic wand again. The swan disappeared as quickly as it had come and there stood Hansel once again.

They were nearly home and just as the evening shadows lengthened and the sun began to sink, they arrived at their door. They rushed in and found their father sitting alone in his old chair. He was overjoyed at their return and the tears flowed down his kind old face as he wrapped his arms about them. Since he had left them in the forest he had not had a moment's peace. Such was the sorrow he felt at doing his wife's bidding that his heart had broken.

As for his wife? One day her stony heart had stopped beating and she had died. The woodsman had not shed a tear for her but since her death

had lived a solitary life, alone with his grief for his lost children.

Hansel then emptied out his pockets and Gretel did the same. The jewels and pearls tumbled on to the floor; the gold and silver coins chinked and clinked as they too fell all around, gleaming and glittering in the last glow of the evening sunset.

The woodsman's tired old eyes opened wide with amazement – they were rich at last! And from that day on their troubles were over and they lived happily ever after.

The Frog Prince

LONG AGO THERE LIVED A KING and queen who had a very beautiful daughter. She was, however, very selfish and thought only of herself. Nothing in the palace held her interest for long and she was often very bored.

One day all this changed when the king gave her a present. It was a golden ball and such was the princess's delight it became her favorite toy. She would play all day in the palace garden, throwing the ball high into the air and catching it as it fell back down to her.

She seemed never to tire of her game until, one bright sunny morning, she skipped out of the garden and wandered into the nearby wood. Up and up went the golden ball as she sauntered along, and snatch and catch went her delicate hands as the gleaming ball fell down again. Ambling through the trees, she came presently to the banks of a stream that bubbled into a deep pool at her feet. Up once more went the golden ball but, alas, the princess misdirected her throw and the ball fell down with a splash in the middle of the pool. Slowly it sank into the depths and disappeared.

"Humph!" said the princess petulantly and leaning far out over the water she peered into the pool – the ball was nowhere to be seen.

She grew impatient and began to bemoan her loss, getting more cross by the minute. "Oh really! Now what am I to play with? I only like my golden ball and I can't even see it!" She looked again into the deep waters but still she could not see her treasured toy.

"I'd willingly give up all my fine clothes and all my jewels, in fact, everything I own, if only I could get my ball back." Her voice grew angry and she stamped her foot.

Suddenly, as she stood beside the stream pouting, a frog poked his head above the water. "Princess, why do you look so glum?" he asked. "What is the matter? Your temper quite disturbed me."

The princess looked disdainfully at the frog, then she told him what had happened.

"Well," said the frog, "I can help you, but you may keep your fine clothes and all your jewels. In fact, I seek no reward save that you learn to love me and let me live with you; promise that I may eat at your table and sleep on your pillow and I will dive down and fetch your precious toy."

The princess raised her eyebrows scornfully. "What nonsense!" she said. "A frog living with a princess? Whatever next! And that she should *love* him? I do declare!" Then the princess remembered the golden ball and such was her desire to retrieve it that she said to the frog: "Very well, it will be as you wish, I promise."

Instantly the frog disappeared and returned within seconds with the golden ball in his mouth; he laid it at the princess's feet.

She gave a cry of delight and snatched up the ball. Then, quite forgetting the frog and her promise, she ran off towards the palace.

The frog hopped on to a rock and called after her: "Princess, come back! Have you forgotten your promise?" But she was gone, his call was in vain and she did not hear him.

On the following day the king and the queen and the princess sat down to dine. As they did so there came a knocking at the door. Tap, tap, tap! They stopped eating and looked across the room. Tap, tap, tap! There it was again, but this time it was followed by a small croaky voice:

> *"Open the door my princess dear*
> *It is your own true love stands here.*
> *Remember the promise you made to me,*
> *Beside the pool, beneath the tree."*

The princess stood up and strode towards the door.

"A frog, m'lady," said the footman as he opened the door. The princess had quite forgotten her encounter by the woodland pool and she drew back in alarm at the sight of the frog.

"Shut the door," she ordered. "Immediately!"

"Anyone we know?" asked the king, "You seem a trifle alarmed, my dear."

"No! Only a horrid frog!" said the princess. "I lost my ball in a pool and he retrieved it for me. He made me promise to love him; to let him live with me, eat with me and sleep upon my pillow."

The king raised an eyebrow and the queen looked over her spectacles.

"I never dreamed of such a thing happening," went on the princess. "But now he's here to claim his promise."

> *"Open the door my princess dear*
> *It is your own true love stands here.*
> *Remember the promise you made to me,*
> *Beside the pool, beneath the tree."*

The frog was knocking on the door again and the princess bit her lip. The king put down his knife and fork: "I think you ought to let him in," he mused. "After all, a promise is a promise and it seems a bit rude to leave him standing on the doorstep." The princess nodded reluctantly and once more the footman opened the door. "The frog, m'lady," he announced solemnly.

The frog hopped to the princess's side. "Pray lift me up to the chair that I may sit by you." The princess did so.

"And, sweet princess, place your plate a little nearer, that I may eat with you." The princess pushed her plate closer towards the frog. He ate heartily and at last, when he had had his fill, he turned to the princess and

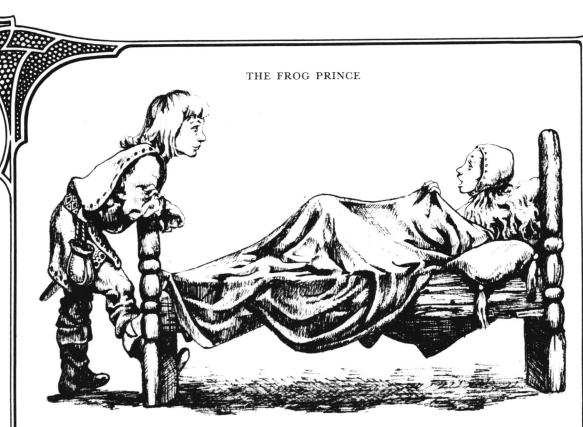

said: "Splendid! Now I am tired. Pray carry me to your bedchamber that I may sleep on your soft feather pillow."

The princess took a deep breath, picked up the frog and walked from the room. She went to her bedchamber and placed the frog beside her on her silken pillow. In the twinkle of an eye he fell into a deep peaceful slumber.

The next morning, when the princess woke up, the frog was gone.

"Thank goodness!" she said. "Now perhaps he will trouble me no more." But she was mistaken: that very same night she heard once more the tap, tap, tap at her door. When she opened it the frog hopped in and slept again on her pillow.

On the third night the same thing happened again, but this time, as dawn crept into the bedchamber, the frog was nowhere to be seen – he had vanished! The princess opened her eyes and turned to see if the frog was lying next to her on her pillow. Then, looking round, her mouth dropped open in surprise for, instead of a frog, a handsome prince stood smiling down at her from the foot of her bed. Noting his good looks and fine clothes, the princess regained her composure and smiled at him demurely.

He began to speak and his voice was soft and gentle. He told a strange tale of a wicked witch who had cast a spell on him, transforming him into a frog. The spell was such that he would forever have the form of a frog unless a princess allowed him to spend three nights on her pillow. "Now," said the prince. "You have broken the spell and by so doing have returned me to my true form." He smiled and took her hand. "Even as a frog I grew to love you, for I had never seen such beauty as yours. Now my love for you is true and my thanks eternal. My greatest wish is that we should marry and live forever in my father's kingdom."

All the time the prince had been speaking a strange warmth had been creeping into the princess's heart. Somehow she felt different: she no longer felt cross at the world and its ways, nor did she feel bored.

"Perhaps," she murmured softly. "There are spells we are not aware of, perhaps these, too, have been broken." She looked up into the prince's dark eyes. Already she felt a deep love for him and she gave her assent to his wish.

All was arranged for the marriage and a fine carriage was drawn up in front of the palace. Six white horses bobbed their heads and waited to take the happy couple away to their new home. The king and queen beamed with happiness, as did the servants – all, that is, except the footmen who were much too important to smile on duty.

The prince led his beautiful bride down the wide sweeping steps and gently took her elbow to assist her into the carriage. But, at the last moment, he hesitated: releasing the handle on the door, he tapped lightly on the coachwork panel.

> "I'll open the door my princess dear
> It is your true love standing here."

The princess laughed and reaching up on tiptoes, kissed him.

Rumpelstiltskin

ONCE THERE LIVED A MILLER: he was not too bright and not too rich, but he did so want to get on in the world. He would tell his friends the tallest tales of how clever he was; how much gold he had, and how many fine clothes he possessed. Unfortunately no one ever saw his oft-proclaimed wealth for no one was ever invited into his house. What little money he had was spent on clothes, to impress his neighbors, but they never quite looked right; his legs were too short and his belly was too fat, so nothing ever fitted. Try as he might he never managed to look like a proper gentleman. He did, however, have one very important asset – he had a very beautiful daughter!

Now it happened that one day the king was passing by close to the millhouse. The miller rushed out, bowing and scraping, with his shirt bursting out behind him from underneath his bulging waistcoat. The king paused, but his eyes were not on the miller but on the miller's daughter who was standing by the door.

When he perceived the king's attention, however, the red-faced miller smiled the more. As usual, he said too much, and before he could stop himself he blurted out: "Yes, my lord, a fine girl indeed . . . and so clever! Why, she can even spin straw into the finest gold."

The king was not impressed with the bragging miller's tale and looked disdainfully down from his horse. "My good fellow, that is surely a rare talent! Tomorrow you must bring her to the palace that I may witness your amazing claim."

The miller gulped – what had he said now! But just as he was bade he took his daughter the very next day to the king's palace. The girl stood patiently before the king while her father fawned and feinted, doffing his cap so often that his wig became lopsided on his shiny bald head.

Ignoring the miller's constant chatter the king stepped down from his throne and led the girl to a chamber filled with straw in which stood a

spinning wheel and a pile of bobbins.

"Now spin this straw to gold," he commanded. "If, from now till dawn, you cannot use all the straw and turn it into gold, then you will die." He closed the door and locked her in.

The miller's daughter was beside herself with anguish. She had not the slightest idea how to spin straw into gold and in despair she burst into tears. How could she justify her father's stupid claim!

As darkness came, her sobbing continued unabated. Then, quite suddenly, the door sprang open and in scampered a strange little man. "How now, my pretty miller's maid, why do you weep so woefully?"

The miller's daughter dried her eyes. "I've to spin this straw into gold by dawn or I must surely die, and truly sir, I have no way to do it."

The little man busily hopped from one foot to the other.

"We'll see, we'll see . . . what can be done. What gift will you give if I spin the straw to glittering gold?"

"You may have my necklace," said the girl raising her delicate hand to her throat. Without more ado the little man leaped to the spinning wheel and sat himself down. Round it flew and round again, and then once more a third time. There – in front of him was a bobbin of gold! All through the night the wheel whirled round and round and didn't stop till dawn when all the straw was gone and in its place was shining gold.

When shortly after, the king unlocked the door, his mouth fell open in surprise. So much gold, he thought, what a treasure have I found in this fair maid. Such wealth was easy to come by, and more was for the taking. That evening he took the miller's daughter to a much larger chamber, again it was full of straw and there sat the spinning wheel and bobbins. He repeated his command of the previous day and once more locked her in. Again she wept but this time not for long, for no sooner had dusk

descended than the little man appeared. "How now, what pleasing present will you give if I spin the straw to strands of shining gold?"

The maiden raised her milk-white hand. "This gold ring upon my finger," she answered. At once the little man set to work, the wheel whirling round and round through the night until the very last strip of straw had been spun into gold.

The king was delighted with the night's work. He clapped his hands and had all the gold bobbins carried to his coffers. But his greed for more had grown even stronger: if the maid continued with her work forever more, he'd surely be the richest king in all the land. He straightaway ordered that the great hall be cleared and filled instead with as much straw as it would hold. It was the largest room within the palace and it took nearly all day to fill it up with straw. The wheel was placed inside the door and the miller's daughter again locked in for the night. She sat within the great hall, pensively thinking on the king's last words. "Tomorrow," he had said. "If all the straw is spun into gold by dawn, then I will make you my wife . . . you will be my queen."

"Fancy?" she murmured. "A humble miller's daughter – a queen!" But then, for the third time the little man appeared before her and asked, as usual, what she would give him for his work. The miller's daughter was forlorn and when she spoke her voice was merely a whisper. "Alas sir, I am sorry, but I have nothing left to reward you for your labor."

The little man scratched his head and raised his bushy eyebrows. "Well now, my miller's maid, this is a puzzling problem. But you'll be quickly queen and then, perchance, a child you'll cherish. Your promise I will take – the baby born will be mine!"

"I cannot say that it surely will be," she answered softly, "but if it happens to be so, then you have my promise."

Once more the spinning wheel whirled and the straw flew through the little man's nimble fingers. Soon the entire hall was shining with piles of gleaming golden bobbins.

In the morning the king was as good as his word: finding all the straw gone and the great hall full of gold, he gave orders for a wedding feast to be prepared. He would marry the miller's daughter.

They lived happily in the palace and the king had so much gold that he no longer asked his wife to sit and spin – besides, he had run out of places to store it all.

A year passed by, and then another, and the queen gave birth to a child – a baby daughter. The child was so delightful that she instantly became the apple of the king's eye and the queen's heart was full of joy. But just three days after the child's birth, she remembered her promise to the strange little man. Hardly had the thought entered her head when he appeared in the room beside her.

"A promise promised is a promise kept," he said. "You must now give me the child. The queen began to weep and begged him not to take the baby girl, offering instead to give him all the riches she possessed. The tiny figure just repeated his request, but her pathetic tears softened his heart and he relented.

"Three days have I waited, so three more shall you have. Within that length of time – today, tomorrow and the third – you must find my name. Should you guess right the pretty princess will be yours."

The queen was greatly comforted by this reprieve but her heart beat wildly as she wracked her brain to remember all the names she'd ever heard. The little man returned that very same evening and asked her for her thoughts.

"Is your name John, or Jack, or is it Lancelot?" she asked, but to each and every name she mentioned the little man solemnly shook his head.

The next day the queen asked her servants what names they knew and sent guards to scour the countryside; they were ordered to seek out every name that ever was. Again the little man appeared at dusk and bade her speak his name.

"Is it Aaron, Arnold, Arthur, Axel . . .?" Again he shook his head.

The third day dawned, it was the last, and the queen felt in her heart that all was lost. However, one of her guards had traveled far away to the mountains. He went straight to the queen to tell her of a strange occurrence he had witnessed close by a lonely cottage.

Outside the house a fire blazed and dancing around it was a strange little man, hopping from one foot to the other. The guard had concealed himself behind a thicket to watch yet not be seen and the little man had started to sing. He sang the same song over and over again, and his words had made the guard prick up his ears.

> "I'll bake and brew, tomorrow too,
> But then, princess, I'll come for you.
> It's such a shame the queen can't claim
> That Rumpelstiltskin is my name!"

It must surely be him thought the queen when she heard the guard's news and she thanked him warmly for his help. That evening the little man appeared for the last time.

"How now, good queen, what is my name?"

The queen pretended to be puzzled and pulled thoughtfully at her lip. "Be it James? Or is it Robert? Be it Gabriel or Ben?" She spoke lightly and waited for the little man to shake his head. He did so and she smiled.

"Then it must be Rumpelstiltskin!"

The little man's face grew purple with anger and he clenched his little fists together and jumped up and down in a fearful rage. "Who told you? Who told you? It surely was the devil!" His temper boiled and boiled and he hopped up and down so wildly that he began to fall to pieces. Each piece in turn hopped about and flew in all directions – through the door and out of the windows: and, from that day to this he's never been seen again – nor, for that matter, have any of the pieces.

The Sleeping Princess

THERE WAS ONCE A KINGDOM FAR AWAY ruled by a very kind king and his equally kind wife, the queen. They lived in a fine palace of courtyards and colonnades, ballrooms and balconies, turrets and terraces, and all day long it hustled and bustled as people went about their business. Although there was much scurrying to-and-fro the king and queen were often lonely as they had no children.

One day, while the queen was walking in the palace garden, she passed close by a small stream. To her surprise a fish suddenly poked its head above the gurgling water and spoke to her.

"Good morning, your majesty," he said cheerfully. "Please, do not look so sad. If you wish for a child your wish will soon be granted – you are to have a baby girl of your own."

As quickly as he had appeared, so the fish vanished, leaving the astonished queen standing there open-mouthed. However, the fish was right, and not long after, the queen gave birth to a beautiful baby girl.

The king was so delighted with his enchanting new daughter that he decided to give a great feast in her honor. Invitations were dispatched to the far corners of the kingdom – to all his friends and relations and the noblemen of the court. He also wished to invite all the fairies who lived within the magic glades of his forest. Their powers would bestow good fortune on his child throughout her life.

But, to the king's dismay, he had invited so many people that he was left with only twelve golden dishes for the fairies to eat from, and there were thirteen fairies! One of them would have to be left out.

The day of the feast arrived and one by one the twelve invited fairies came to the palace. Each had brought a special gift for the princess: one brought virtue, one brought beauty, another brought riches, and yet another brought wisdom – and so on until the little princess was endowed with all that is excellent in the world. Eleven of the fairies had bestowed their gifts when suddenly a dark figure stepped forward from the crowd. It was the thirteenth fairy who had not been invited to the feast. She was cold with anger and her eyes blazed with revenge at being slighted. She began to speak and her voice was heavy with malice.

"This princess will thrive, but not for long, just until the day of her fifteenth year. Then, she will be wounded by a spindle and she will die!"

The assembled gathering was stunned and silent. To wish for such an evil thing to happen was unthinkable. But then another figure stepped forward – it was the twelfth fairy who had not yet given her gift to the princess.

"Let me now give my gift," she said in a soft voice. "I cannot stop this evil spell from taking its course, but be assured, the princess will not die. Should she be injured by the spindle she will fall asleep, but alas, her sleep will last for one hundred years."

The king was beside himself with fear and gave orders that every spindle in the land be destroyed immediately lest the threat come to pass. Not one spindle must remain to injure his precious daughter.

The years passed and the fairies' gifts were fruitful. The princess grew more beautiful each day; she was well-mannered and amiable; her kindness was beyond compare, and her wisdom and honesty made all who knew her love her more.

At last, however, the day of her fifteenth birthday arrived. The king and queen had left the palace to search for a special present for their daughter and she was left alone for the day. Feeling a little bored she wandered through the halls and chambers of the palace seeking amusement. She discovered rooms she had never seen before and came at last to the foot of a winding staircase that twisted up to the top of a tower. She daintily ascended and as she climbed the stairs it began to get dark and gloomy. At last she reached the top and there, set in the keyhole of an iron-studded door, was a golden key. The princess reached out and turned it and the door sprang open. In front of her sat a little old lady quietly spinning at her wheel.

"Why, good mother, how came you to be here?" asked the princess pleasantly. "And what is it that you do with so pretty a wheel?"

The old woman smiled and rested from her work. "I am spinning, my child. Do you not know how it is done?" And she rose and passed the spindle to the princess.

"How enchantingly the wheel spins," said the princess, laughing happily, but hardly had she uttered the words when she felt a sharp pain in her finger. The spindle had sorely pricked her – instantly she slumped from the stool and fell lifeless to the floor.

The prophesy had come true. However, the princess was not dead but only sleeping, but then an even stranger thing took place. The king and queen had just returned to the palace and had begun to search for their daughter: at the very moment the spindle had pierced her finger they too fell asleep. So did the courtiers and the cooks, the footmen and the guards, the kitchen cats and the courtyard dogs – in fact, every living thing within the palace fell into a deep slumber.

Time passed by and a great thicket of tangled thorns grew up around the palace completely hiding it from view. No passers-by could see beyond the dense wall of briar and thorns and in time the palace and its occupants were almost forgotten.

A few old men remembered the story of the beautiful princess who slept within the enchanted castle and passed the tale down to their sons. Many princes and noblemen had heard the same tale and sought to find this unknown beauty within her sleeping castle – but all had failed. Some had given up their search at the first sight of the tangled bushes and vicious spiny thorns. Others had struggled through for a few yards only to find themselves trapped, and, snared within the thicket, had perished where they lay.

Many more years passed and there came to those parts a king's son. He had been hunting close by and stopped to spend the night at a lonely cottage. The old man who lived there did not have many visitors and was pleased to have some company to talk with. He told the prince about the hidden palace, lingering over the story, stopping and starting and puffing on his old pipe. The prince listened patiently and when the old man described how beautiful the princess was, his eyes opened wide with interest.

"I think, old man, that I will seek out this maiden, and if she is as fair as you tell, then she will be my wife."

The old man drew in his breath and laid down his pipe. He also remembered his grandfather's warning: of many such daring adventures and many princes and noblemen who had died in their efforts to seek the sleeping beauty.

"Take care, my son," he said kindly. "Not one brave man has yet lived to tell of the maiden's beauty. The thorns are so thick that all have been ensnared and perished." The old man was fearful for the young prince's life and went on: "Pay no heed to my words. It is just an old man's foolish story."

The prince was not deceived and made up his mind to seek out the enchanted castle as soon as dawn broke. He bade farewell to the old man and set out on his way. It was three whole days and three nights before he came upon the wall of thorns. There he stopped and set up his camp to wait for morning, thinking long into the night on how best to cut his way through the spiny barrier.

By great good fortune the morning of the fourth day marked the end of the one hundred year curse. When the prince opened his eyes the wall of thorns had vanished. In their place was a wild abundant growth of sweetly perfumed flowers. True, they grew to a great height and were sprouting thickly in all directions but they would not prevent the prince's progress. The prince passed through them with ease but as he neared the castle the forest of blooms closed up behind him as thick as ever, leaving no trace of his path.

At last he felt the solid stones of the courtyard beneath his feet. He could hardly believe his eyes: there were the sleeping dogs, while on the roof slept doves with their heads beneath their wings. In the kitchen sleeping cooks rested by their pots, and guards and footmen lounged, snoring, in all the halls and chambers. He came upon the two great thrones and saw the sleeping king and queen – nothing stirred, all was quiet. He wandered on through the silent castle and every breath he took sounded in his ears. At last he came to a staircase leading to the upper floors of the palace and he bounded up without delay. At the far end of a long passage he came to the door of a small bedchamber. He entered and there was the maiden sleeping peacefully on her silken pillows. She was indeed of such serene beauty that he could not take his eyes off her. He bent and gently kissed her lips.

Instantly the princess opened her eyes and looking up, she smiled at him. He took her hand and led her from the chamber. The palace yawned and all about them people began to stretch and wake up. The king and queen, the courtiers and the cooks, the guards and the footmen, the dogs and the cats and even the pigeons – all were waking as if they had fallen asleep only the previous day.

The spell was broken. The prince declared his love for the princess and she, in turn, agreed to be his wife. The king called for a great feast to be held and from that day on they lived happily ever after.

Rapunzel

THERE ONCE LIVED A MAN and his wife whose dearest wish was to have a child of their own. For many years they lived with their sorrow but at last there came a day when their hearts were filled with joy – their wish was to come true.

The house they lived in was set high up on the side of a steep hill. From the tiny window at the back of the cottage, they could look down over sweeping grassland into a neighboring garden. They did not know who owned it, nor who tended it, but its beauty was matchless. All through the year, whatever the season, it blossomed in a profusion of delicate and colorful plants. Flowers of all description grew abundantly amid leafy shrubs and sweet-smelling herbs. Strangely, the garden always seemed to be bathed in sunlight – no cloud ever appeared to shade its beauty.

The man and his wife would spend hours sitting by their window admiring the garden; marveling at the array of color and blossom; sifting the sweet perfumes that drifted up the hillside towards the cottage, filling the air with a delightful fragrance. They had never been able to see the garden close-up for it was surrounded by a high stone wall. They had both walked around this wall several times but the only entrance they could find was a great solid iron door, deeply studded with heavy bolts and set soundly within the stonework.

As the time for the birth of their child drew near, the man's wife retired to her room at the top of the house. Her only diversion was admiring the garden and savoring the perfumes that wafted up to her from its many plants. Among them was the unmistakably tangy aroma of wild chives, and as time went by, this scent alone seemed to possess her. She scanned the garden from her high vantage point and finally saw the crisp green shoots growing close beneath the high wall. As day followed day her desire to taste their flavor grew stronger and stronger – she began to think of nothing else. She refused all other food, so obsessed had she become at

the thought of eating chives. At last she became so weak that her health
began to fail and her poor husband feared for her life. She begged him,
her voice thin and frail, to fetch her some chives to eat. So great was his
alarm that he agreed to her request.

So, one dark night, the man crept out of the cottage and stole through
the shadows towards the garden wall. Placing a ladder against it he
clambered over the top and dropped silently to the ground on the other
side. A sudden chill breeze caused him to shudder as he stood in the
darkness. Then, as his eyes became accustomed to the strange gloom, he

bent and quickly plucked an armful of the succulent chives. Seeing a nearby apple tree pegged to the wall, he scrambled up through the branches and climbed down his ladder. He made his way safely back to the warmth of his cottage.

His wife was overjoyed when she saw the bundle of chives her husband had collected and she quickly prepared them as a delicious salad. She smiled contentedly as she savored their flavor, delighting in their crispness. However, their taste lingered on her palate and when she had finished eating, her desire for more became greater. She prevailed upon her husband to return that very night and replenish her plate. The poor man was tired and weary from his exertions but promised he would go back to the garden the following night. Reluctantly, his wife accepted his promise and slept, her head full of dreams of the fresh taste of chives.

Once more the man set out toward the garden and a shiver of fear ran through him as he drew close to the dark wall. Once more he clambered up the ladder and swung his legs over the top of the wall. He was about to drop down to the other side when the moon came from behind a cloud and lit up the garden in an eerie glow. The man hesitated for a moment, then, dropping to the other side he quickly tore at the chives with his heart pounding. Suddenly the moon lit up the scene again and the silver chives at his fingertips were, in the same instant, shrouded by a long black shadow.

Startled, he looked up and a chill ran down the length of his spine – standing above him was a tall hooded figure. The moon drifted behind the figure's head and it grew even blacker against the heavy night sky. The man could not make out the features of the face beneath the hood at all, but then the figure spoke.

"Why do you steal from my garden?" The voice was low and tinged with evil and the man shivered. It was the voice of a sorceress.

"I . . . I . . ." he stammered. "My wife . . . she would have died but for the taste of these tender chives." He nervously thrust the torn shoots towards the dark figure.

The figure swayed as if moved by the night breeze and was silent for a long time. Then, as if appeased, leaned closer over him and spoke again: "If that is so, you may harvest my plants as you so desire."

Still the man could not see the face that spoke and he trembled and shuffled to his feet. Even standing, the figure towered above him and when next it spoke its voice had dropped to a barely audible whisper.

"But there is one condition," the figure hissed. "When your wife gives life to the child within her . . . it will be mine! I will take it as my own – the child will prosper and its advantages will be great within my domain."

The terrified man nodded his head anxiously. "Yes, yes, I promise, the child will be yours!"

Not long after, the child, a baby girl, was born and the very same night the sorceress appeared and took her from her parents. She held the baby close in her arms, turned from the cottage door and drifted into the shadows. The man and his wife heard her footsteps stop and then from the darkness came an evil voice: "Now she is mine – she will be called Rapunzel."

Rapunzel grew into a beautiful child; her skin was as clear as the petals of a rose and her long silken hair was as golden as spun sunlight. She was happy and carefree but one day, when she was twelve years old, the sorceress called her from the garden where she was playing. She took her by the hand and led her into a deep wood. There, she was shut up in a tall tower which had neither steps, nor door, nor any entry save a small window set high up in the stonework at the top.

Time went by and Rapunzel would sit at the tiny window and watch the seasons passing by. The sorceress would come each day to visit; she would stand beneath the tower and call up to the maid: "Rapunzel, Rapunzel, let down your hair."

The maid would hear the call and twist her hair, which during her stay in the tower had grown amazingly long, around an iron hook set in the window-sill. Then she would cast her silken tresses down to the ground below. The sorceress would clasp Rapunzel's hair and scramble up.

Now the king who ruled those parts had a son and one day he happened to be hunting within the forest close to the tower. As he rode between the trees a strange sound reached his ears, beautiful and pure, a maiden's voice singing sweetly like a bird in spring.

At first the prince could not decide which direction the singing came from, but he rode on and presently drew his horse up beneath the tower. It soared above him into the treetops and though he rode round and round it he could find no way to enter. The enchanting song still filtered from the tiny window high up at the top. The prince was beside himself with curiosity but finally, in despair, he turned his horse away and went back to his father's palace.

Thereafter he returned each day to sit beneath the tower and to listen to the maiden's song.

This became the prince's habit and the long days of summer drifted into autumn. One warm afternoon the prince was sprawled beneath a beech tree when he was suddenly startled by a sharp croaking voice. Looking toward the tower he saw a tall black-clad figure cupping a pair of bony hands to its mouth. "Rapunzel, Rapunzel, let down your hair."

The prince shuddered at the harsh cry. He crouched down and hid himself in the long grass. As he watched a cascade of golden hair fell from the window and the black figure, clutching wildly at the silken tresses, clambered roughly to the top of the tower.

"So," thought the prince. "If that's the way to enter the tower, then I too will wait until dusk and enter. Then, perhaps, I will find the maid who sings so sweetly."

The shadows lengthened and the prince watched the sorceress depart. He crept from his hiding place and strode to the tower. Looking up he called softly: "Rapunzel, Rapunzel, let down your hair." In an instant the long golden hair fell down within his reach.

When the prince swung himself through the window opening Rapunzel drew back in fear, never had she seen a man before. However, his kind manner and soft words reassured her and she was soon calm again. He was astounded by her radiant beauty and grace of movement. Never, in all his life, had he seen such an enchanting maiden.

Rapunzel smiled as she listened to his tale; of how he had come each day to listen to her song and sit beneath the tower; of how he had been

desperate to catch a glimpse of her face; and of his foreboding whenever the sorceress appeared. As he spoke her soft smile captured his heart and he fell deeply in love with her. He dropped to one knee and asked for her hand in marriage.

Rapunzel had listened to his speech and was equally charmed. She thought how handsome he was and how kind were his words. He would surely care for her more than the wicked sorceress, and treat her with love and affection. She reached out and placed her hand in his, consenting to his wish.

"Gladly would I leave this place," she said, "and travel with you wherever your wish would take us. But, my love, there is no way for me to escape from this high tower. I cannot climb down these fearsome walls."

The prince looked thoughtful for a moment, then his face brightened and he began to speak again in a low voice. "Each day," he began, "I will bring a skein of silk to you. From the threads you must plait a silken ladder. When it is complete you can climb down and leave this cursed place forever."

"I will do as you say, my dearest. Together we will ride away and live in happiness until we die." It was agreed.

The sorceress came only during daylight hours, so, when the shadows grew long, the prince would steal quietly to the tower and leave Rapunzel with a skein of silken threads. For a while all went well and the ladder she plaited grew longer and longer. One day, however, the unsuspecting sorceress tugged so hard at Rapunzel's hair that the maid exclaimed without thinking: "Good mother, how is it you are so much heavier than the king's dear son. He is as light as a feather and does not tug my hair so roughly."

The sorceress's eyes grew wide with anger and she flew into a rage at Rapunzel's words. "What's this I hear!" she screamed. "How dare you betray me, you wicked child! You'll pay for your deceit!" She sprang at Rapunzel and seized the maiden's hair close to her brow. Pulling it angrily, her rage continued: "Did I not set you here to keep you from the world. You belong to me, and only me . . . and only I will look upon your beauty!" Then, taking a knife from her belt, she slashed at Rapunzel's golden hair, severing it in one mighty blow.

Rapunzel's fate was sealed. The old crone blindfolded her and spirited her away from the tower to a far-off land. A land of sand and flints where no living thing could thrive – a land of misery and wretchedness.

That same evening the sorceress returned to the tower to take her revenge on the impudent prince. Inside the tiny chamber she took up Rapunzel's severed hair and wound it tightly around the iron hook in the sill. Then she sat back and waited for night to fall.

The last rays of the sun vanished and sure enough, as they did so, she heard the prince's call: "Rapunzel, Rapunzel, let down your hair." The golden tresses tumbled from the window and the prince sprang lightly to the window.

He entered the room and there, to his horror, found himself staring into the wild flaming eyes of the evil sorceress. There was no sign of his beloved wife, Rapunzel. The old crone had let her dark hood fall from her head and her hideous face was contorted with rage.

"So," she scoffed. "You have come for your beauty, have you?" Her voice was as brittle as broken bones. "Well, she has gone . . . forever! She'll sing for you no more, my proud lad. The wild cats will drag her off, tear out her hair and pluck out her eyes. Your love is lost for all eternity!" Her voice rose to a frantic screech and she laughed with madness. She advanced towards the prince.

Her words had stung him with sorrow and his heart was almost breaking. The evil cackling laughter rang through his tormented mind. In despair he turned away from the grotesque creature and flung himself from the window.

Down, down he tumbled, surely to his death, but his fall was broken at last as he fell deep within a thorn bush. His life had been spared but not so his sight: the needle-sharp thorns had pierced his eyes and he was blind.

Three long years passed and the prince, now ragged and alone, stumbled aimlessly through the forest. It had become his home and he lived by eating the wild berries from the shrubs and roots plucked from the forest floor. Some were sweet to the taste and some were bitter but he no longer cared, so great was the sadness in his heart at losing his beloved wife.

At length his wanderings led him far from the shelter of the forest. He staggered far out into a land of desolation; a plain of crumbling rocks and flints that cut him sorely. He searched for food, but cut his hands on barbarous thorns – not one thing could he find to eat.

At last, exhausted and weak from hunger, he slumped down to rest against a boulder. He rested his weary head back against the warm rock and closed his eyes. It was as if he were dreaming: the world seemed to swim round him and pictures floated through his head. Sounds flowed through his tormented mind, and one was like an angel singing. The voice was sweet and far away and it reminded him of something long ago. The voice seemed to draw nearer and he realized it was no longer a dream. It was Rapunzel's voice!

Wildly he staggered to his feet and ran towards the singing, only to fall cruelly among the vicious flints. "Rapunzel, Rapunzel," he called. "Where are you?" He stumbled on once more, but then, quite suddenly, he stopped. A soft hand restrained his arm and reached to touch his brow.

"Oh, my dearest love," the voice was as sweet as he remembered it. "It is you!" Rapunzel flung her arms about him and wept with joy. She could feel his thin shoulders through his ragged coat and her tears flowed even more. They washed his cheeks and moistened his eyes as he clung to her.

A faint haze danced before him and a brightness invaded his brain. More of her tears flowed into his eyes and his vision began to clear. At last he saw before him his long lost love, Rapunzel. Beside her were her twin daughters – his children, and each with golden hair.

His arms encircled them and through his own tears he drew them to him and felt the warmth of joy return to his heart.